Parent's Introduction

We Both Read is the first series of books designed to invite parents and children to share the reading of a story by taking turns reading aloud. This "shared reading" innovation, which was developed in conjunction with early reading specialists, invites parents to read the more sophisticated text on the left-hand pages, while children are encouraged to read the right-hand pages, which have been written at one of three early reading levels.

Reading aloud is one of the most important activities parents can share with their child to assist their reading development. However, *We Both Read* goes beyond reading *to* a child and allows parents to share reading *with* a child. *We Both Read* is so powerful and effective because it combines two key elements in learning: "showing" (the parent reads) and "doing" (the child reads). The result is not only faster reading development for the child, but a much more enjoyable and enriching experience for both!

Most of the words used in the child's text should be familiar to them. Others can easily be sounded out. You may find it helpful to read the entire book aloud yourself the first time, then invite your child to participate on the second reading. Also note that the parent's text is preceded by a "talking parent" icon: ; and the child's text is preceded by a "talking child" icon: .

We Both Read books is a fun, easy way to encourage and help your child to read—and a wonderful way to start your child off on a lifetime of reading enjoyment!

We Both Read: The Old Blue Hat

—————————————————————

We Both Read® is a registered trademark of Treasure Bay, Inc.

Published by Treasure Bay, Inc.
40 Sir Francis Drake Boulevard
San Anselmo, CA 94960 USA

PRINTED IN SINGAPORE

Library of Congress Catalog Card Number: 2001 132689

Hardcover ISBN-10: 1-891327-37-2
Hardcover ISBN-13: 978-1-891327-37-7
Paperback ISBN-10: 1-891327-38-0
Paperback ISBN-13: 978-1-891327-38-4

We Both Read® Books
Patent No. 5,957,693

Visit us online at:
www.webothread.com

WE BOTH READ®

The Old Blue Hat

By Dev Ross

Illustrated by Meredith Johnson

TREASURE BAY

"There's no one to play with!" Max wailed one bright and sunny afternoon. His mother shook her head and told him he wasn't going to find a friend just sitting around all day!

So Max trudged off to see what he could find. And there, sitting on the sidewalk in front of his house, Max saw . . .

. . . an old blue hat.

"Wow," said Max. "What a cool looking hat!"

He bent to lift it when suddenly—WHOOSH— the hat blew away, bouncing and skipping off down the street.

The hat finally came to rest in front of his neighbor's house.

The hat was on a can.

"I've got you!" said Max as he reached for the hat. Then all of a sudden, the hat went "meeoow."

Max jumped back and wondered what was **under** the hat! Then the hat lifted slightly and out poked a nose.

Under the hat was a cat.

"A friend!" Max exclaimed, delighted by the sight.

The cat yawned a huge, lazy yawn and Max thought it made her look just like a **lion**!

"We can play circus," he said with a smile. "I can be the ringmaster."

"You can be the **lion.**
We will do tricks."

Max pretended to stick his head into the lion's huge mouth. He pretended he could see all the way down to the lion's tonsils.

Then Max stepped back to shout his next command.

"Jump, lion, jump!
Jump on the drum!"
But the cat just sat.

Max tried several more tricks, but the cat wouldn't **play.** She just jumped off the can and walked away, her tail waving lazily.

The cat did not want
to **play.**
This made Max sad.

Then the wind snatched the old blue hat right off of Max's head. WHOOSH—it went tumbling down the street again. "Where would the hat go **next**?" he wondered.

Max chased it down the sidewalk.

Max saw the hat land.
He saw it land **next** to a dog.

Max grinned when he saw the dog. This dog's name was Pete and he was Max's friend.

"Will you play with me, **Pete**?" Max asked the pup.

"Woof!" barked Pete as he held the hat up to Max.

🔵 **Pete** did want to play.
He gave the hat to Max.
But Pete did not let go!

Pete and Max played tug-of-war and it was tons of fun. Then Max thought of another game.

"Let's pretend that this hat is a terrible blue monster," said Max. "Then we can be the super heroes who save the **world**!"

Pete gave a happy bark.
He wanted to save the
world.

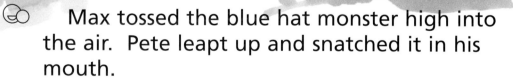

Max tossed the blue hat monster high into the air. Pete leapt up and snatched it in his mouth.

"Good job, Pete," shouted Super Max.

"Woof, woof," answered his super dog **friend**.

"It is fun to save the world," said Max.
"It is fun to have a **friend**."

Super Pete brought the blue hat monster to Super Max. The blue hat monster was just about to escape again when suddenly the super heroes heard a whistle.

It was Pete's owner, calling for his pup to come **home**.

It was time for Pete to go.
It was time to run **home**.

Max tried saving the world without Pete, but it just wasn't the same without his super friend.

Then Max tossed the hat a little too high and . . . WHOOSH!

A big wind came.
It took the hat.
Max ran to get it back.

Max found the hat on a patch of grass. When he reached for it, the hat hopped high into the air! Max grinned as the hat hopped again. It looked like the old blue hat had suddenly grown two long, skinny, green legs!

But the hat did not have legs.
It was just a frog.

Max introduced himself and asked the little frog if he had a name.

"Riiibbiit," said the frog.

Max shook his hand and said, "Nice to meet you, Ribbit."

"I hope you like to play," said Max. "We can play with my blue hat."

Max sat beside the frog, held his hat like a steering wheel, and began to **drive**. He pretended that they were speeding down a winding raceway in the fastest racing car in the whole wide world. No one could beat them! They passed cars on the left. They passed cars on the right.

Max let the frog **drive**.
The frog drove well.

Max and Ribbit were winning the race! They were going to earn the delicious grand prize! Varoooom—they headed for the finish line!

Then the frog saw a bug.
Now he did not want to drive.
He went to get the bug.

Max watched his frog friend hop off into the distance. "I'll never find a friend today," said Max. "I might as well give up and go home."

Then Max heard a voice behind him. The voice said . . .

"I like your blue hat."
Max looked up and saw
a boy. Max smiled and
gave him the hat.

The boy put on the old blue hat and tried to act like a grown-up. That made them both laugh!

Then the boy told Max his name was Tim and wondered if Max would like to play ball with him.

Max could hardly believe his ears. Did someone just ask if he wanted to play?

"Yes, Tim," said Max.
"I want to play!
I want to play with you!"

Max and Tim ran down to the park. They pretended that they were famous baseball players, playing the last and most important game of the World Series!

Tim and Max had lots of fun. They played all day. They made plans to play the next day.

Max found a wonderful new friend on that bright and sunny afternoon. And he did it with the help of . . .

 . . . an old blue hat.

If you liked
The Old Blue Hat, here are two other
We Both Read ® Books you are sure to enjoy!

A wild ride of imagination awaits every reader of this Level 1 story for beginning readers. Aunt Sue takes her niece on a ride of adventure that brings them to some places you can only find in a book! There's a store with clothes that have cats and pans in the pockets, a park with jogging frogs, and a zoo that is run by the animals!

To see all the We Both Read books that are available,
just go online to **www.webothread.com**

A very whimsical tale of a boy and his dog and
their fantastic dreamland adventures. This delightful
tale features fun and easy to read text for the very
beginning reader, such as "pigs that dig", "fish on a
dish", and a "dog on a frog." Both children and their
parents will love this newest addition to the We Both
Read series!